53 SMILES

53
Special Moments
In Life's
Exquisite Simplicity

Philip J Bradbury

"... this is a short and thought-provoking read. The stories are written with care, creativity and utilising strong descriptors which immediately draw in the reader. An enjoyable collection of stories!"

~ Tia Mitsis, author of *A Greek Odyssey*

Tessy pouted as she packed her toothbrush, Sandy doll, brush set and colouring pencils and went downstairs to make a peanut butter sandwich for lunch. Then, while daddy mowed the back lawn, she stalked off to mummy's house, defiantly, uncertainly ... not the last time she'd leave a man to ease her pain.

In 1953 the Queen was crowned, Everest was climbed and I was born. In celebration of that momentous occasion, I created this book of 53 53-word stories. Actually, the first sentence is correct but the second isn't. I entered a Flash Fiction contest, wrote my 100 words and didn't win. Knowing that nothing is for nothing and everything is for a reason, I pondered my loss for 3 days and then decided to write 53 53-word stories, each to go with a sign I'd photographed over the years. Why 53? No reason, really. It just sounded a nice number. Then I remembered my birth year and knew, absolutely, that this was divinely inspired and my wise and humorous words would be read and admired down the ages. Actually, that's not quite truthful, either. It was a nice change from writing 80,000-word books for the writing was soon done. But don't let the shortness of words fool you - they're deep and they deal with topics

53
Special
Moments
In
Life's
Exquisite
Simplicity

Philip J Bradbury

we don't like to talk about - killing, suicide, abuse, death, ageing and judgement, sadly. They're also about nicer topics - humour, forgiveness, kindness, miracles, walruses and seagulls, happily. There's also true stories and stories of life and how to live it without fear and with effectiveness. Strangely, as some have found, something may just happen in your life that is echoed in these pages, something that gives you a clue to get through an improbable drama, an intransient problem or a pesky person. The variety of stories ensures there's something for everyone with a fascination about how life works, what we do to make it not work and how to have it working better. Those realisations can come from humour, horror or a simple sigh of acceptance. Be gentle with this book and with yourself. Both deserve another look, another chance and another smile. You didn't arrive on this planet to live in misery and fear. This book may help you see life differently and to live it peacefully. That's my hope.

QUIET PLEASE

LIFE IN

PROGRESS

The world is a wasteland, waiting for our creativity; an insanity waiting for our peculiar and particular brand of creative sanity.

The crucible of aliveness is on the edge of madness and in the throes of unshakeable and solid knowing – beyond belief – of the unknowable; experienced in the smallest moments and deathliest silences.

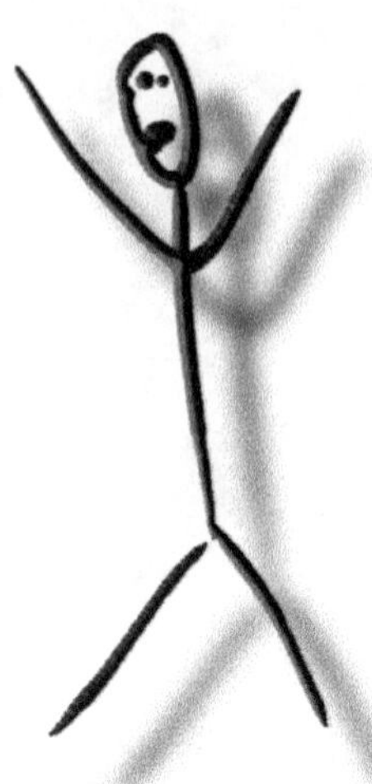

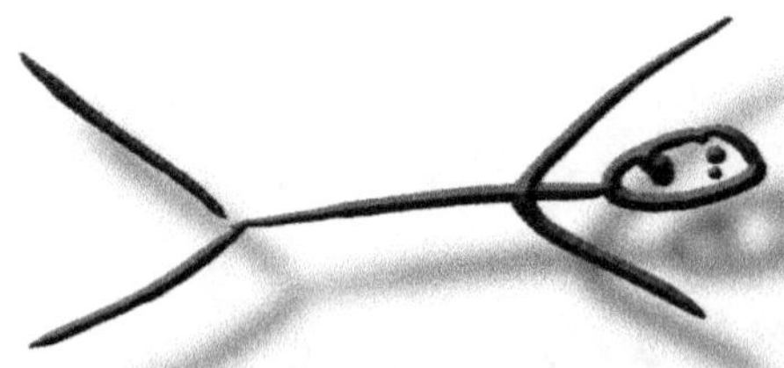

I keep missing my father.

But my kind neighbour,
who has experience in
these things, has been
teaching me how to keep
my emotions steady, to
focus properly, to stay
calm and to breathe
evenly.

So, next time my dad
hits my mum I, with
my neighbour's new
pistol, won't miss my
father.

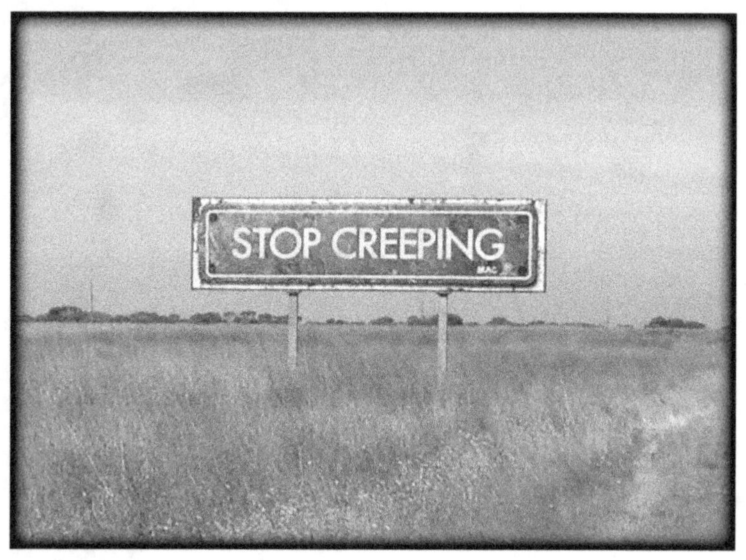
STOP CREEPING

Buffalo Joe couldn't walk a straight line or afford another drink but he talked up a ragged story.

They scoffed at his mad murder story in their town ... till they found the policeman's wife slain, the next morning, and her husband gone.

Judge not a story by the stagger but the substance.

CAUTION
Road Works

Be tolerant

No one listened and no one believed poor Fiona, save Eric, who opened his hands to collect her tear drops and cradle her falling heart. She had nothing he wanted save that she was another human.

He loved flesh back onto her naked, uncertain bones by listening, by simply being there.

Nothing more.

DON'T EVEN
THINK OF
PARKING
HERE

Enjoying their romantic meal, a woman nearby started coughing, choking and turning blue.

He leapt up, raised her up, lifted her skirt, whipped down her panties and licked her bum. Shocked, she gasped, coughed and breathed again.

"It works every time," he said to his girlfriend, as he returned, "that Hind Lick Manoevre."

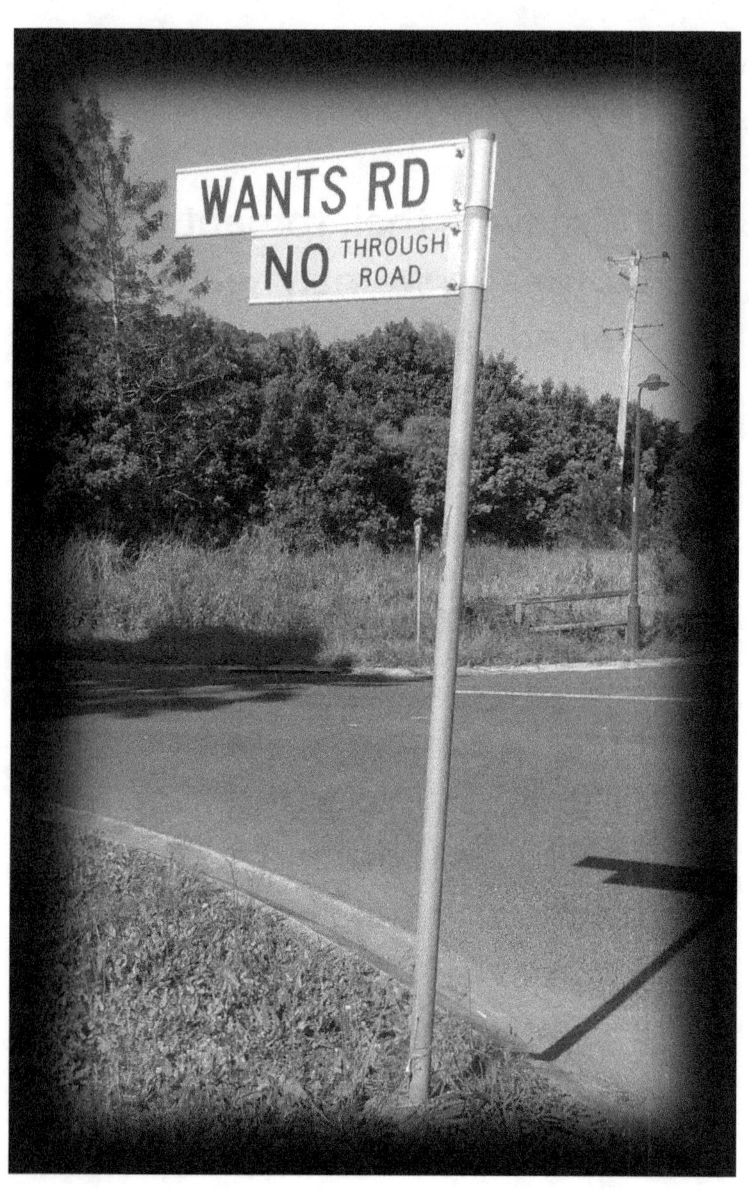
WANTS RD
NO THROUGH ROAD

He collapsed, glimpsed blue sky for one last time, from the hospital bed, and wondered if it was worth it; the fighting, dealing, grasping, acquisitions, businesses and lost loves.

His hearing, the last sense to close down, faintly heard his family squabbling over his immense assets. Releasing and grasping continued their relentless cycle.

SOLDIERS RD
NO EXIT
AA

OH, GLORY AND REWARDS FROM HIS COMMUNITY WHEN THE SOLDIER STRODE OFF TO KILL PEOPLE HE DIDN'T KNOW; PEOPLE WHO CRIED OUT IN A LANGUAGE HE DIDN'T KNOW TO A GOD HE DIDN'T KNOW ... TILL HE AND HIS COMMUNITY CRIED OUT TO GOD WHEN HIS HOUSE WAS BURGLED.

MY, HOW GLORY FADES!

This would be a blank page if I hadn't just told you it was! Your thoughts on that, in 53 words?

CAUTION

No man, save Ed, looked Patsy in the eye for her breasts rose high, proud and inviting. No man, save Ed, held her body for he, alone, saw through the valley of temptation to a mind sweet, bright and loving.

Where bodies join, first, all is cleaved. Where minds join, all will come.

SPEAK
FOR
THOSE
WHO
HAVE
NO
VOICES

Ian was bigger than his wife but just couldn't hit the woman when she came at him with fists and saucepans. Mates and police laughed; something about being a real man.

Choosing between being abused and missing kids, he did neither.

They believed the step-father but Ian had hanged himself two years earlier.

Memory Lane
LEFT 150 m

Another cold, early day; lurch into business suit, boring breakfast, stumble into car for a two-hour gridlocked push to work.

Another day of mindless meetings and smiling like I'm coping. I'm not.

Another day over and then stumble into car for a two-hour gridlocked push home, boring dinner and TV.

Another lifeless day.

LOST
VERY LOST

"Tuwitteewoo," said the sparrow, landing on the cow.

"Moomoodeloo," said the cow, any old how.

"Doggydedoo," said the dog, lifting his leg somehow.

"Zipzipadedoo," said the lizard, licking her brow.

Most of our words are gobbledegoo and nobody understands anyoldhow. But it does feel good making noises with others.

We call it connection.

WORLDS END HWY
Robertstown 30
Eudunda 52
BURRA CREEK GORGE 10

Unable to destroy the golden bellybutton that made him special, and hate himself, he sat and wept.

A fairy flew in saying, "Lie on the beach at full moon, eyes shut all night."

The next morning, he found the golden bellybutton was gone. He leapt up with joy and his bum fell off![1]

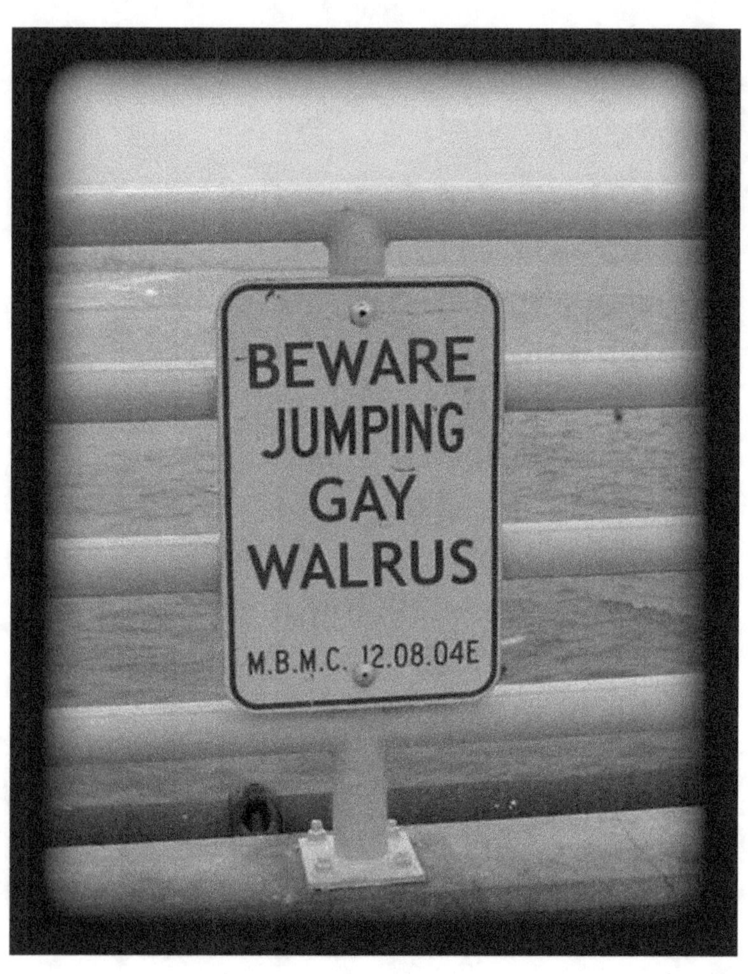
BEWARE
JUMPING
GAY
WALRUS
M.B.M.C. 12.08.04E

Watching a walrus while his whiskers gwow and weach out to tickle you in wicked ways is weaweing. He wears a sewious face 'cause that's how he's made – a mask so solemn, it's weally hard to tell he's welaxed.

Be aware, my wayward friend, happy people may wear wowwied expressions and wise wersa.

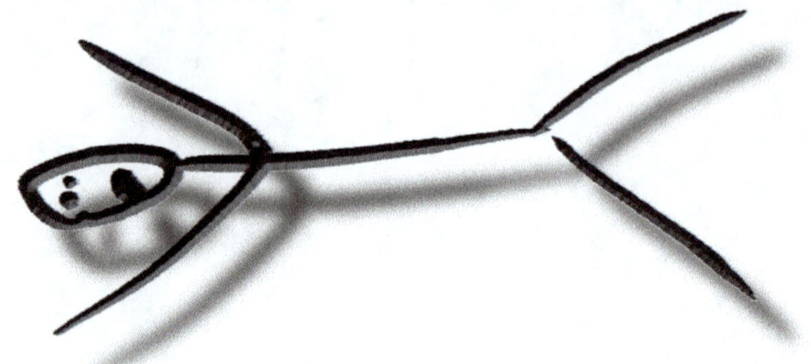

Closing his eyes, he pretended to sleep, pretended sickness, for another day. His parents, he knew, were choked with fear for his "sickness".

SH 2 Heaven
Double Passing Lane

Who to please?
Them, to dispel
delusion of his
weakness while he
submitted to another
day of bullying? Or
himself, growing
obese in comfortable
dread?

A fourteen-year
old's daily dilemma.

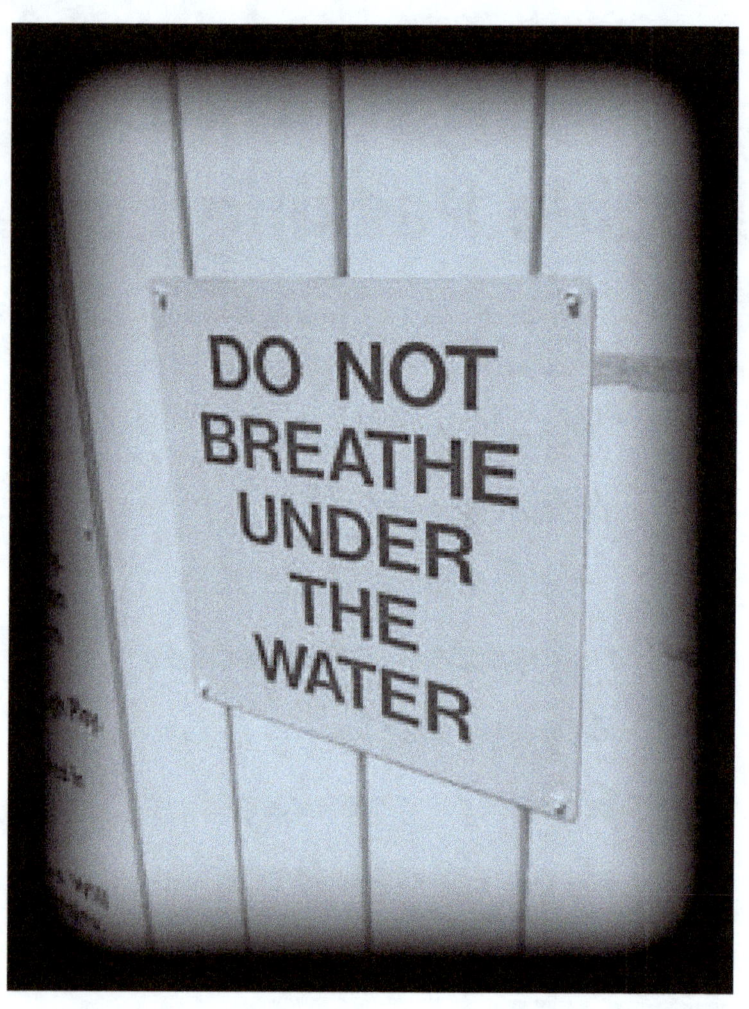
DO NOT
BREATHE
UNDER
THE
WATER

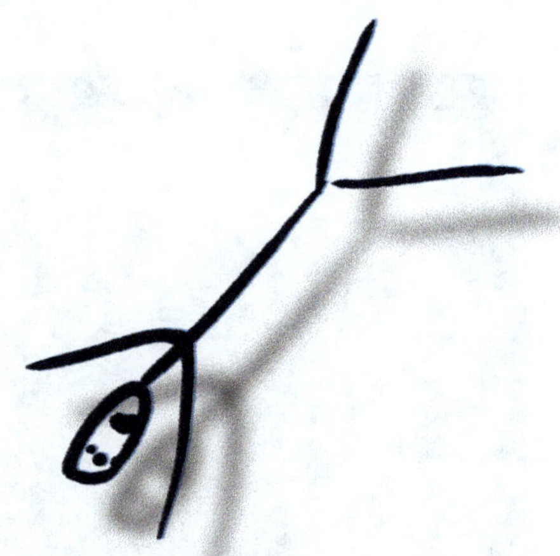

Diving from the cliff, a dozen thoughts thrilled him – excitement, fear, how impressed they'd be, the stories he'd tell.

Then, approaching, he saw the wave receding and knew he'd mistimed it.

Waking from his coma a dozen thoughts shamed on him – frustration, anger, self-hatred, a life less lived and no stories to tell.

REST OR
R.I.P
DRIVER FATIGUE
CRASH ZONE
NEXT 39km
OLD WARES
COLLECTABLES
PLANTS
8 CHARLOTTE ST

Donald knew he was driving fast, tired from the long drive. Pills and alcohol weren't helping and his family missed him.

However, business was business and he'd sort the rest out one day.

He watched, from above, as they buried his body – another traffic statistic – and wished he'd spent more time at work.

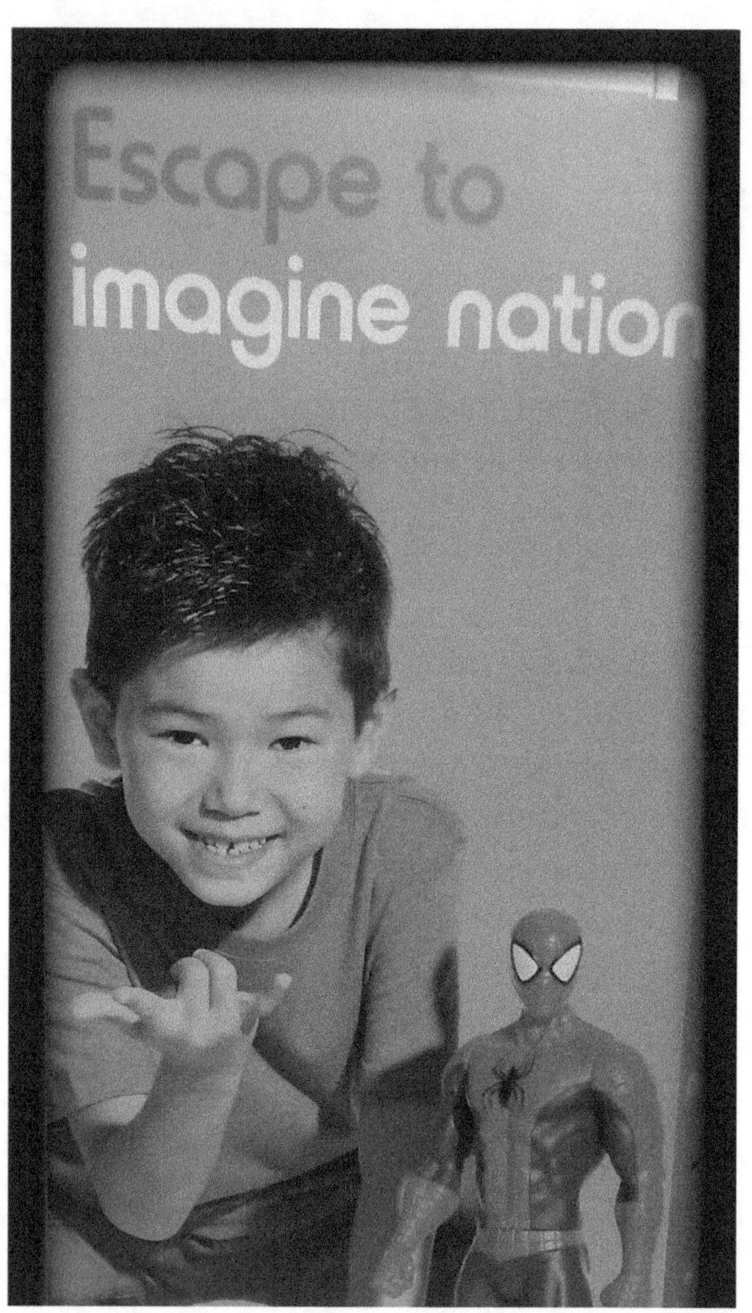
Escape to
imagine natior

"You're upset at being called Old Man?" she asked, incredulously. "Sixty is Old Man to a forty-year old. Twenty one is Old Man to a twenty-year old. Old Man just means you won the Being Born race. You're a winner!"

He suddenly felt okay about being called Old Man. Very okay.

NO PARKING

THIS AREA IS
RESERVED ONLY FOR
GAY
ALL OTHERS
WILL BE TOWED

"How can my son be gay?" he demanded. "After all I've said and done for him?"

"He's like his father," I suggested.

"I'm not queer!" he sneered. "He never listens."

"Exactly!" I said. "Love hears no boundaries."

"That's love?" he snorted. "That's distorted!"

"Love is concerned for another. Just like you are now."

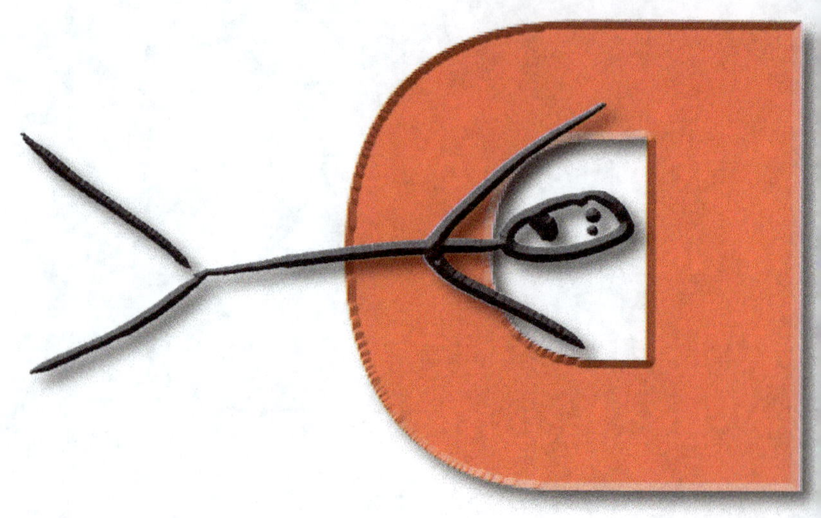

TE

Sounded like he's strangling the toilet then emerges; pale, shaky.

"Good night?" asked John.

"Awesome!"

"Interesting?"

"Drinking. Awesome! You?"

"Meditated. Wrote TED speech."

"Ted who ... whatever. Ouch!" Hand to forehead and stumbled into his room.

John left to commune with awesome TED people and speak to a million.

Same planet, different awesome.

FIRE ENGINE
TURNS

Flicker couldn't fight fires so he'd cry while adult engines saved the town. How to learn but by doing? A little practice fire but the decrepit old station soon burned ...

Flicker
fire-engine's
first
faulty
fiasco
for
fighting
fires,
fortuitously
forcing
funding
from
finance-
fisted
fathers
for
flash,
fireproof,
firefighting
facilities
... a tongue burner!

Prevent your cat
committing a crime
against wildlife
We love cats, but if left to roam they
can kill thousands of native wildlife.
Be responsible: desex and confine your cat.
#Purrfectcriminal
Learn more about living with Australian wildlife at
www.rspcaqld.org.au/livingwithwildlife
RSPCA
Queensland

Phoebe suspected that Tom was unfaithful, despite his protestations of undying love.

Maybe it was his sudden disappearances overnight, maybe it was the smell of others on him, maybe the smell on his breath and she knew someone else had been feeding him.

She just knew because that's just the way cats are.[(2)]

Please
do not feed
the Pelicans

The full bodied pelican glided to the water, feather-light, and rested in quiet stillness.

A yapping dog is scooped up, flailed around the rubbery bill, is tossed aside and runs, panicking, never to approach birds again.

Food is provided by gawking tourists and off he flies; a lesson taught, a reward given.(3)

Don't make me
come down there.
- God
Texas United

"God created the thought that allowed itself to perceive itself as you … as different."

"I *am* different," he sneered.

"Because you perceive differences."

"I have free will, mate!"

"You have free will to align with God in peace or to misalign in anger."

"What's to be peaceful about?" he demanded.

"Perception."

"Huh!"

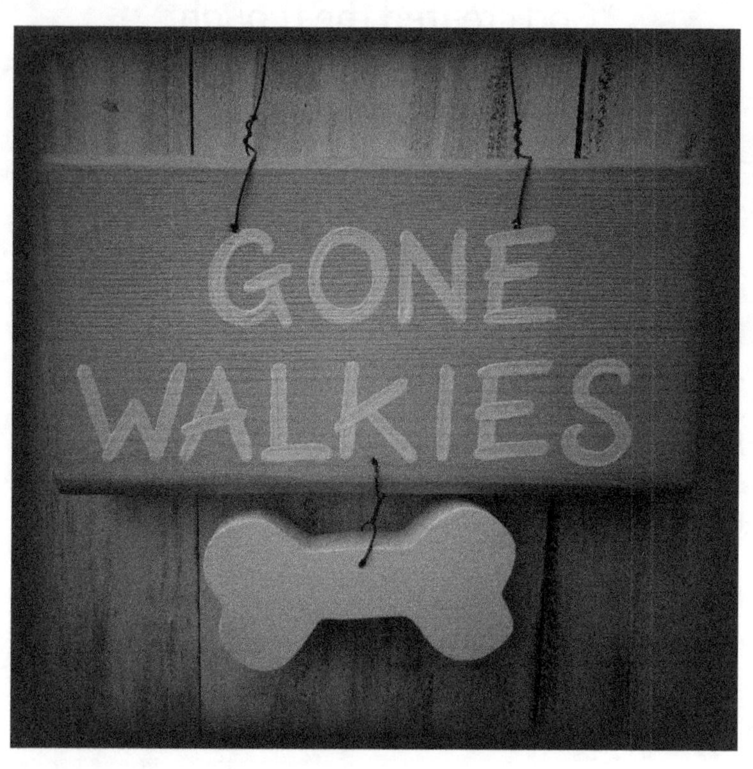
GONE
WALKIES

He wasn't called Stormin' Norman for nothing.

His knees and gut instinct could predict earthquakes, tornadoes and hailstorms days in advance. That's how he was; it was just natural.

But when the scientists, press and cynics arrived at his door, demanding to know how, he was gone.

He had predicted that shower[(4)] too.

QUIET PLEASE!

TEACHING

AND

LEARNING

IN PROGRESS

**Beyond Samsara –
the deathly rattle
of human busyness
– is a compellingness
which is beyond
meagre desire and
social oughtism.**

**It takes us, should
we risk a step into a
bottomless sanity, to
a silence that shouts
down mountains
and calls to mind an
ancient song, so long
forgotten.**

**It brings us back
home.**

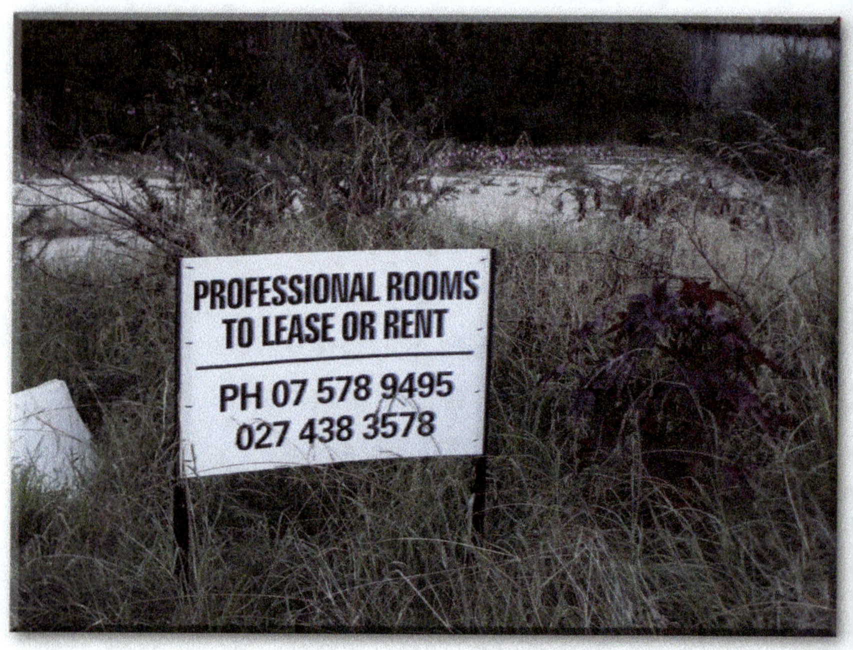
PROFESSIONAL ROOMS
TO LEASE OR RENT
PH 07 578 9495
027 438 3578

Thomas was a farmer through to his bones.

But what to do when his finances finally gave out and he had to sell the farm?

Become a labourer?

Become unemployed?

Retire?

No, all too demeaning and dead-end. He became a farm consultant, making pots of money telling others, "Take my advice; I didn't."

THE HELLISH NEIGHBOURS KEPT US AWAKE FIVE HOURS A NIGHT WITH THEIR NOISE.

AFTER SIX MONTHS, WE LEFT OUR BEAUTIFUL HOUSE FOR A WRECK IN

THE PEACE OF THE COUNTRY.
BUT SHEEP, COWS, BIRDS,
GECKOS AND FROGS KEEP US AWAKE
EIGHTEEN HOURS A DAY ... THE FASTER
WE RUN, THE WORSE IT GETS.

NOTICE
NO SIGNS
ALLOWED
AT THIS
INTERSECTION

A stranger approached. "You are Joe McMahon, fighter pilot of 72 missions, shot down, parachuted to safety and imprisoned by the Viet Kong for six years. I packed your parachute."

We tearfully hugged.

How many others had anonymously saved me? I sat and thanked my wife for "packing my parachute" every single day.(5)

BENALONG ST
ARCADIA AVE

In the cozy of an English pub he accepted another Guiness and explained that, in his Irish village, there were street names but no street numbers.

"So, how would I find your house if there's no numbers?" I asked.

"Oh aye, if ye'd never been dere, why would you ever want to come?"[6]

IF DOOR DOES
NOT OPEN
DO NOT
ENTER

He entered politics to make the world better and soon realised he'd end up resigned, angry, bitter.

Then Betty told him the most sacred place was where an ancient hate turned into a present love. Eventually, haltingly, resistantly, he forgave the world, accepted its insanity and made himself better.

Betty beat the bitter.

THIS SIGN IS IN
SPANISH
WHEN YOU'RE
NOT LOOKING

An Englishman, Spaniard and Italian were chatting, speaking their own languages.

Only the Englishman could not understand the others, pretending he could while the others knew he couldn't. They called him *lunático* and *pazzo* while he indulgently accepted their "compliments".

This won't touch you unless you're being duped by your pretences. Ponder it.

He admired the machine, momentarily, then kicked it into life, the roar and vibration coursing through his bones.

His neighbour looked over in envy – the shine of metal, weight of engine, power within.

He smiled back indulgently, knowing the pleasure of riding was all his. Sadly, his back lawn was too soon mown.

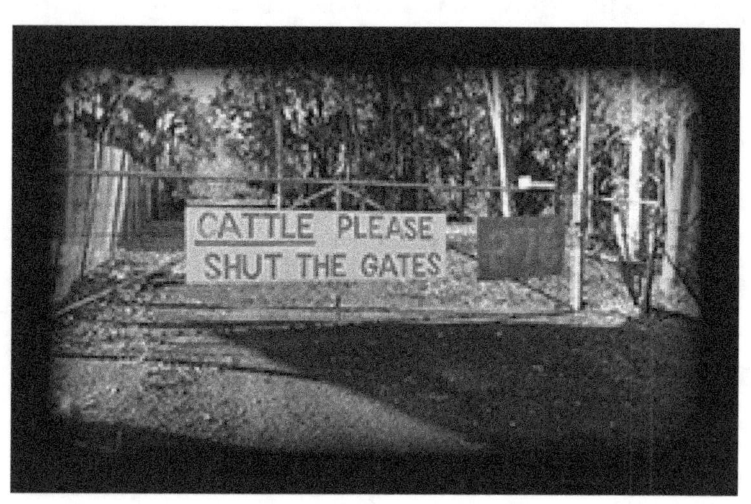
CATTLE PLEASE
SHUT THE GATES

He managed the 22,000 acre property with fierce, creative efficiency, never crossing that gentle line from *good boss* to *good friend*.

Then retirement.

Having avoided interests or friendships – even with family – his sharp mind befriended that soft hole for those with passion gone. Dementia held him as fiercely, creatively, as had his work.(7)

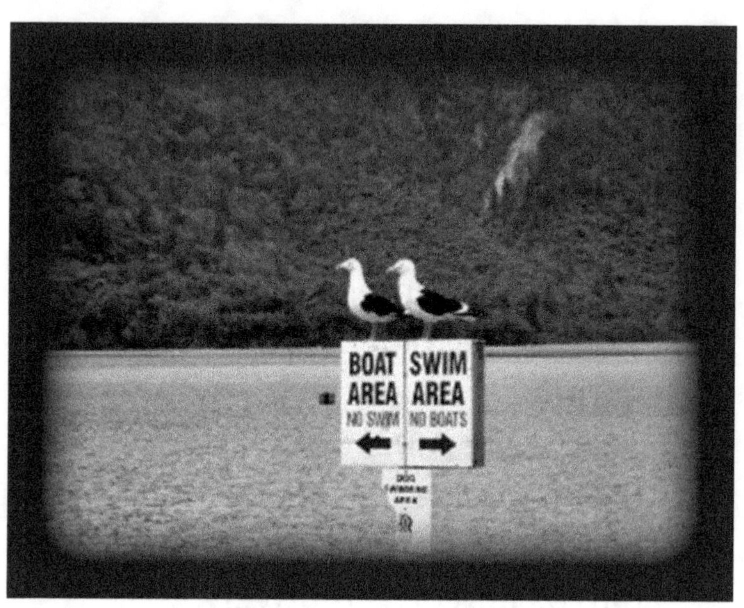
BOAT AREA
NO SWIM
SWIM AREA
NO BOATS

Six times the erratic wind dumped me. I'd kick desperately and haul the windsurfer back downwind, lurch back on board, pull on the mast and sodden sail up again, smiling tiredly.

The seventh time I lay on the board, exhausted, wishing for land. My tired legs flopped ... and found the lake's bottom![(8)]

CAUTION

INCREASED RISK
OF ICE WHEN
LIGHTS FLASH

Everyone knew Ken was Mr Nice. Janice doubted herself because others did. Smiling face during the days he hated, he turned from Nice to Ice with the woman he "loved".

Abuse and slapping grew imperceptibly, and no one was there to listen to or believe her.

Her death was a shock to all.

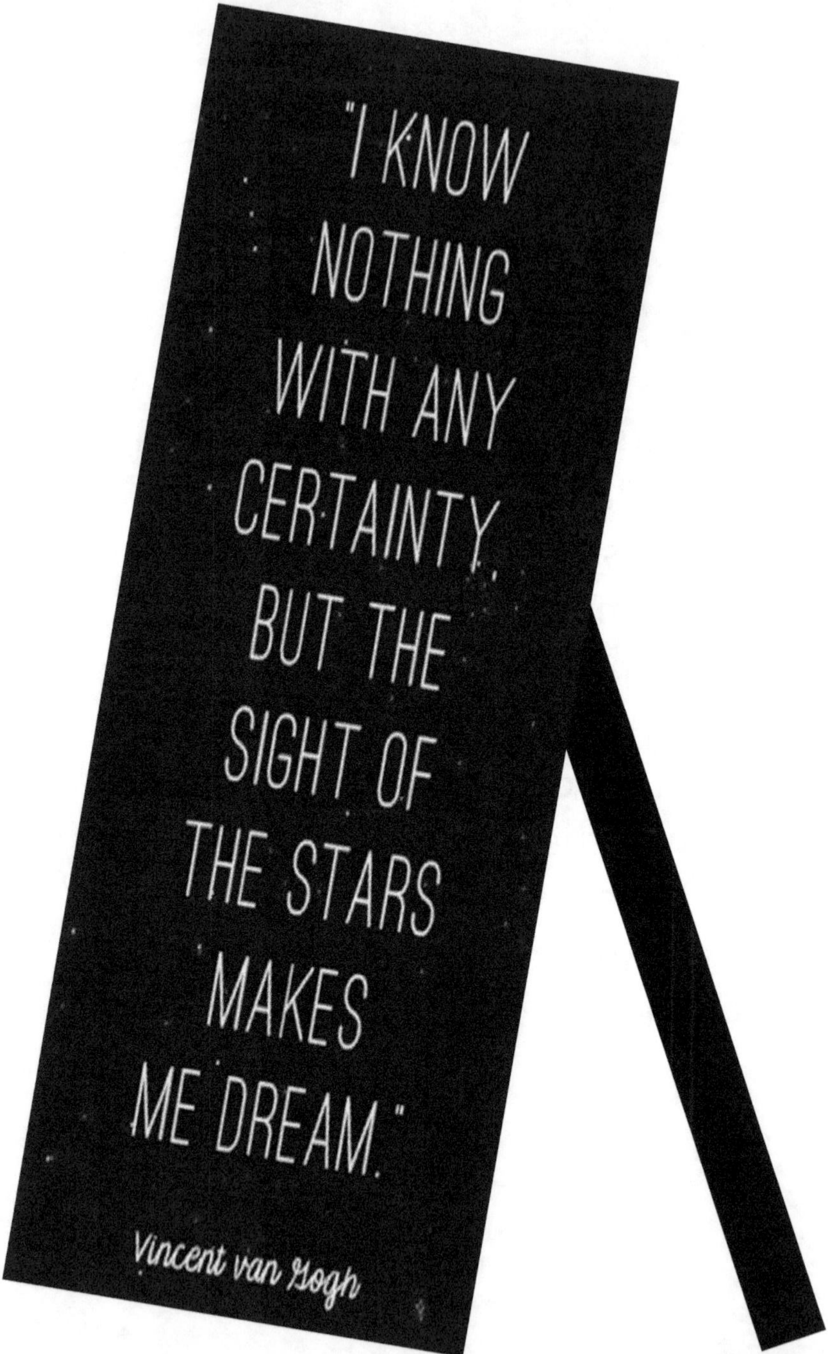

"I KNOW NOTHING WITH ANY CERTAINTY, BUT THE SIGHT OF THE STARS MAKES ME DREAM."

Vincent van Gogh

If any idea was Truth, there would be no discussion, dissention or danger. All would be certainty.

No such idea has ever arisen.

Our conclusion must be, then, that we – politicians, clerics, scientists, mothers, idiots and masters –

Are
Making
It
All
Up

That, darlings, is all the Truth we know .... we don't.

DANGER
BURIED
CABLE
CALL BEFORE DIGGING
YOUR CUSTOM
PHONE NUMBER HERE

Hank dug and found steel cable ten feet down; concluding, scientifically, the Iroquois had telephone lines 300 years ago.

James then found iron cable twenty feet down; concluding, scientifically, the Celts had cable communications over 1,000 years ago.

Then Hori dug ten feet and found nothing; concluding, logically, the Maoris always had wireless.

Surprised by Gestapo, his parents were violently taken; him huddling, hiding, then found by Jewish friends.

He learned surprises were fearful; attracted more darkness. Then, a miracle moment, changed his mind and looked to surprises with glee, against all logic.

Surprisingly, weirdly, glee bounced back. The world turned light and he smiled again.

FORGIVENESS

"You forgive me? Isn't that arrogant?" he asked.

"No, we're all capable of errors," she said.

"So it's okay what I did?"

"It's not okay and I forgive you."

"What's forgiveness then?"

"It means it's not okay but I've released my bitterness."

"We're still friends then?"

"Friends perhaps, peaceful definitely and marriage over."

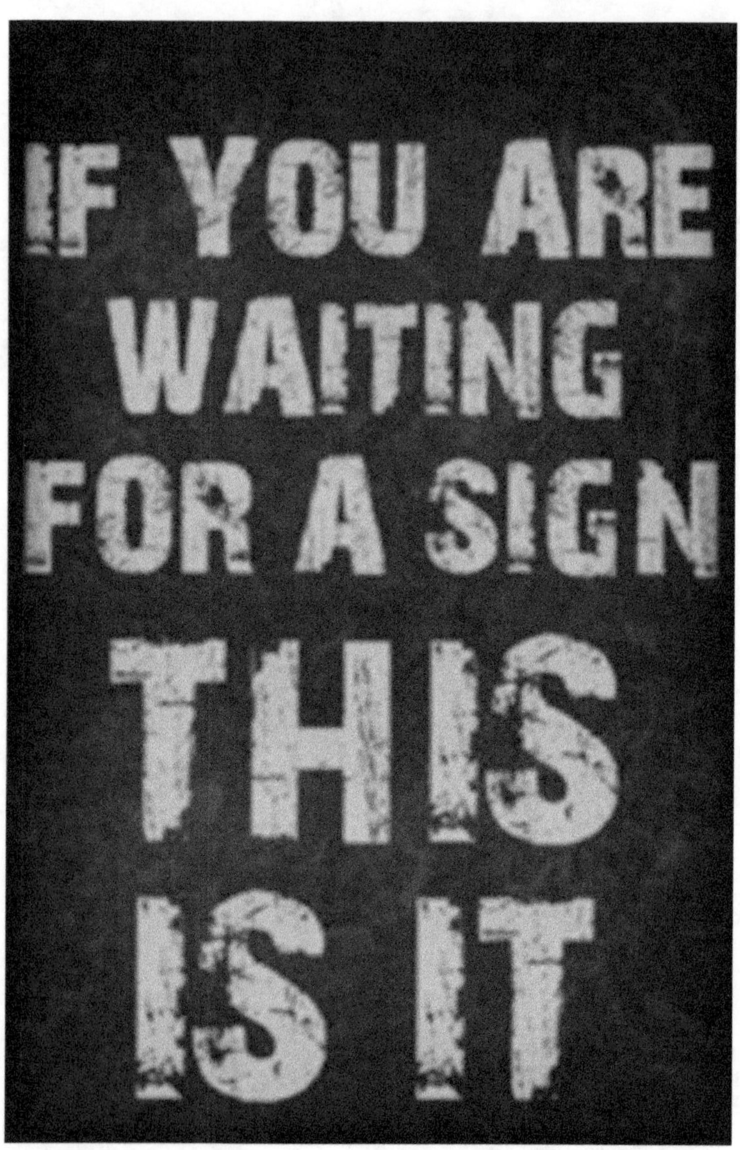
IF YOU ARE
WAITING
FOR A SIGN
THIS
IS IT

The last question – who am I? – cannot be asked from earthly frames.

The first question – how am I not? – is the doorway to the first.

How am I not this fear and guilt? How am I not this judgement and perception?

From these come the experience – not the understanding – of who I am.

ONE WAY
GOOD LUCK
FIGURING OUT
WHICH ONE

If 2,000 women from
  Uncle Sam
  Cross-dress as soldiers in
Viet Nam,[9]
  If a Christchurch cop
named Sam,
  Fired for off-duty
dressing in glam[10],
  If women wear trousers
like a man,
  But men can't wear
dresses, ma'am,
  If girls wear sandals to
the evening jam,
  And blokes' foot
exposure is banned,
  If …

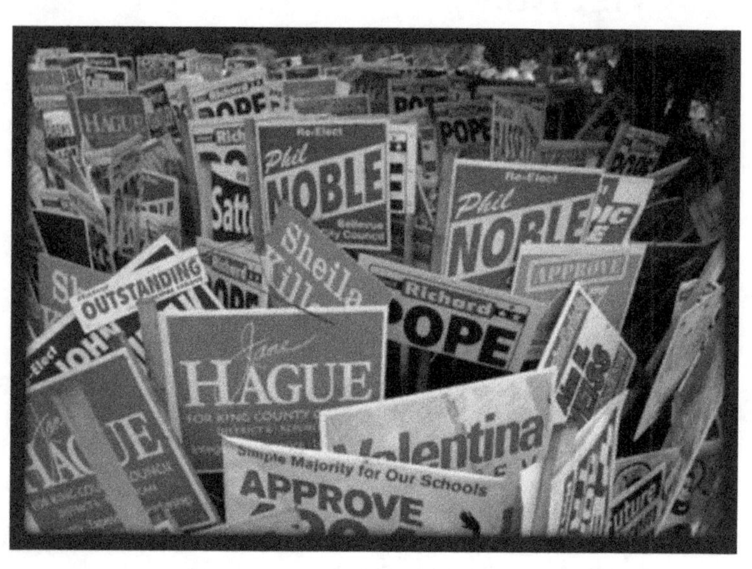
Re-Elect
Phil
NOBLE
Re-Elect
Phil
NOBLE
POPE
HAGUE
OUTSTANDING
Sheila
Richard
POPE
APPROVE
HAGUE
Valentina
Simple Majority for Our Schools
APPROVE

"I've come to change the world for you," said the politician.

"It's fine. Leave it alone," they said.

"But I want to make a difference!"

"Make a difference in your mind."

"But nobody would notice. I'd have no acclaim."

"You'd have peace and respect, forever."

"I want it now."

"Respect yourself then. Now."

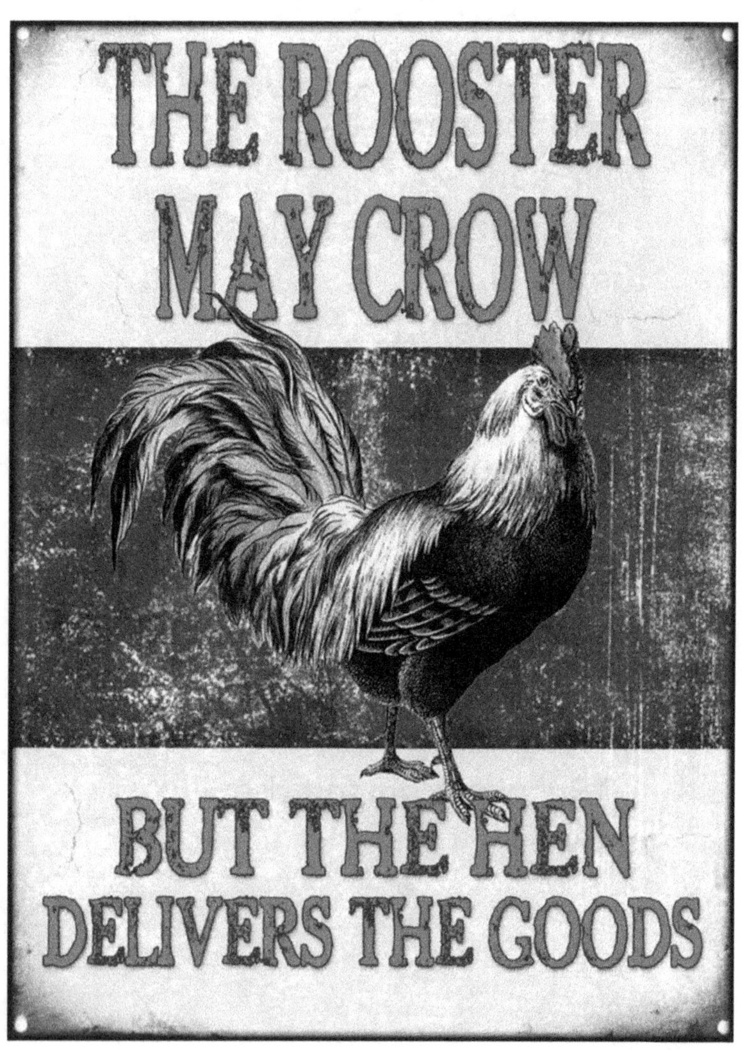
THE ROOSTER
MAY CROW
BUT THE HEN
DELIVERS THE GOODS

"You're the biggest freak,"
said sparrow, pooping on wire,
"You've the biggest cheek,"
said crow, landing on pyre.
"Your brains are mush."
Flying off quick.
"Your brains I'll crush."
Spinning round quick,
Stuck to sparrow poop,
stickiest in poopdom.
"Size means nothing, with
feet glooped on!
"Upside down crowing is
vanity on fire!"

You're four times
It's hard to
more likely to
concentrate on
have a crash
two things
when you're on
at the same time.
a mobile phone.

Heaven Rd

No Exit

He turned from the curb and knew he shouldn't have. A passing truck slammed his car into a wall.

As his wife's voice bleated from broken phone, his concerns flicked to broken bone and bleeding lung. In the snap of a wrist, the "What's she think?" thoughts became "Will I live?"

Priorities changed.

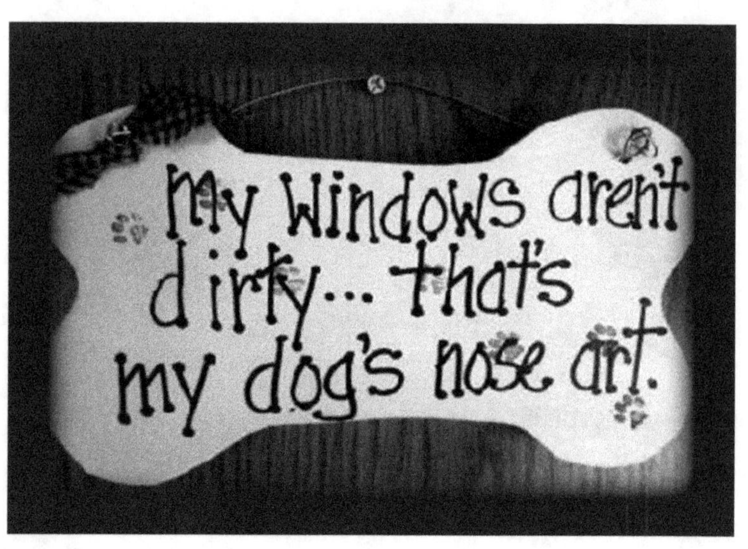
My windows aren't
dirty... that's
my dog's nose art.

Hector stopped, annoying his friend.

He sniffed the familiar scent of Paddy, the grey bearded chap ... whiff of Dolly, nice legs, wiggly bum ... dank smell of jealous Hubert ... mmm, the smell of fear. Obviously an argument.

I miss juicy gossip, he thought, as his human friend tugged on his leash.

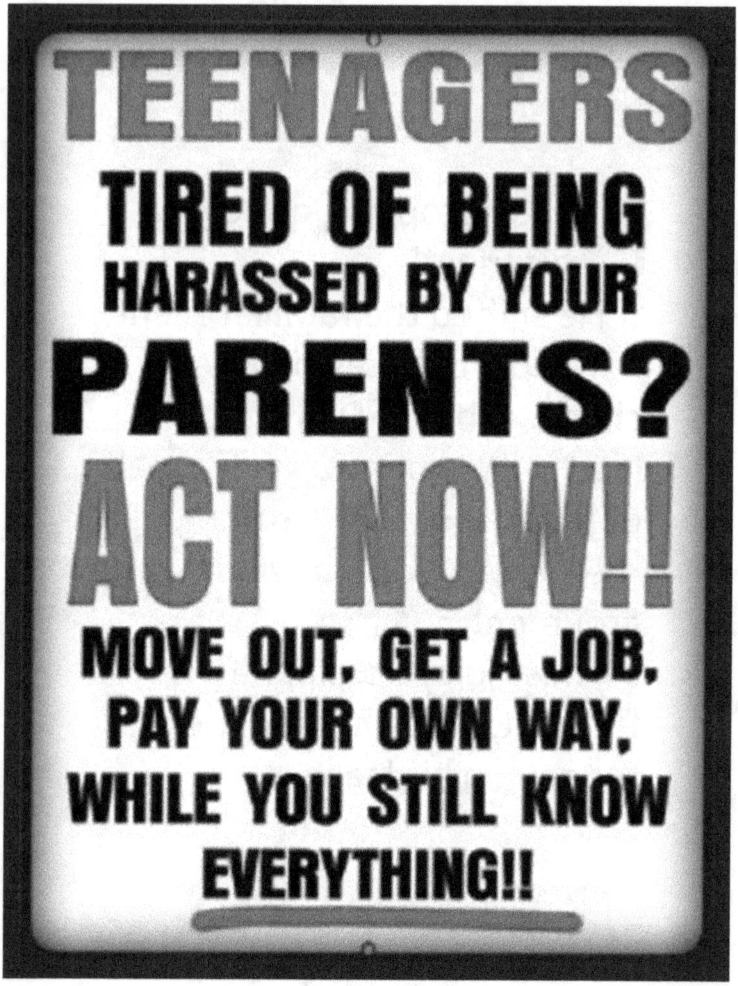

TEENAGERS
TIRED OF BEING
HARASSED BY YOUR
PARENTS?
ACT NOW!!
MOVE OUT, GET A JOB,
PAY YOUR OWN WAY,
WHILE YOU STILL KNOW
EVERYTHING!!

"If it's too loud, you're too old,"[11] the teenagers said. "If it's too scary, you're too chicken,"

To return to a world I invented, life would be so exciting, so full.

Thankfully, I've become old and have dispensed with adrenalin in favour of that which no one invented ... the peace of God.

I closed my mouth and spoke to you in a hundred silent ways

The tiny glistening waterfall erupting from her eyes said, "Forever yes!"

Her sigh enfolded my heart and her warm hand steadied mine as I slid on the ring. My name was safe in her smile and my life was sure in her caress.

Though mute, her eloquence eclipsed all my words could convey.

Keep smiling for, one day, life will grow tired of making you miserable.

It's like a kick in the teeth, winning that $23 million. After spending $6 million on paying debts, buying clothes, pretty toys, new car, motorbike, overseas trip and investment properties, I should be happy.

After the euphoria, I'm back to the familiar feelings of hopelessness and disconnection.

What's it take to keep happiness?

Stupidity is an elemental force for which no earthquake is a match

When the world split, it collapsed and fell aright.

Before the earthquake I demanded that everyone obey my view of what should be and lived in constantly disappointed anger.

After losing everything, I realised I had no control in an insane world. When I accepted what was, I let go and smiled peacefully.

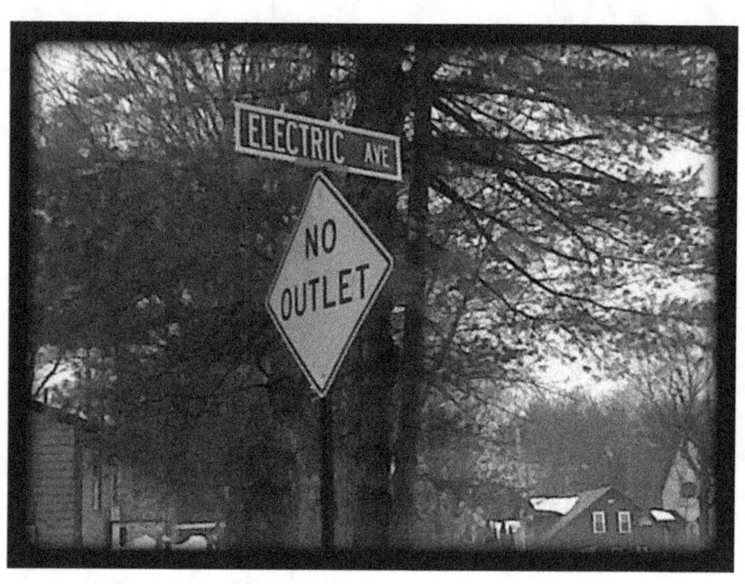
ELECTRIC AVE
NO
OUTLET

She wore her studies like her shoes – loosely, without laces – pretending she was committed and intellectual.

We cannot waste time; Time doesn't care. We can only waste our lives.

After two years she was left with a debt and a failure image, both tied tighter than any noose.

Time for pretending was over.

LAUNDRY TODAY
OR
NAKED TOMORROW

He put the book down and wondered about writing his own ... but 100,000 words would take forever and who would read them?

The idea persisted. He wrote 2,000 words today ... and another till, 100,000 later, he'd completed his book.

Dreaming forever, acting today; one day at a time, his dream emerged.

The hymn to reality is an acknowledgement of the unknowable divinity within us.

Our sacredness sits in trust beyond senses: unseeing and invisible, unhearing and silent, untouching and touchless, uncontrollable and caring master of all.

Though words are inadequate, we ever attempt description of that which meets us with the inevitables of life.

Appendix ...

1. Page 27 - This is the (much) shortened version of the first story in the book, *The Royal Bank of Stories*, and the inspiration for the short novel, *Circle of Gold.*
2. Page 45 - The Australian SPCA - the one organisation that proports to help animals - treats cats as criminals when they break the rules we don't tell them about, whatever they are!
3. Page 47 - I actually saw this at Southport, Gold Coast, Australia ... and laughed my head off!
4. Page 51 - *Shower* is an English colloquial term for a group of idiots.
5. Page 59 - This is a true story.
6. Page 61 - A true story, this happened to me in a pub in England.
7. Page 69 - This is my father's story.
8. Page 71 - A true story as this happened to me on Lake Rotorua, New Zealand - a large but shallow lake, something I'd forgotten!
9. Page 85 - Over 2,000 women dressed as men and fought in Viet Nam.
10. Page 85 - In 1998 a NZ policeman was fired for cross-dressing in his off-duty time.
11. Page 95 - My son once told me, as I complained about the noise level from his room, "Dad, if it's too loud, you're too old!"

Heart ...

In New Zealand I experienced life as an accountant, credit manager, company director, shepherd, scrub-cutter, tree pruner, freezing worker, plastics factory worker, saxophonist, army driver, tour bus driver, stage and television actor and singer, builder, lecturer, facilitator for men's groups, reporter, columnist, magazine editor, publisher, writer ...

In South Africa as an AIDS workshop co-facilitator ...

In the Australian bush as a barman, horse and camel trekker and stock-whip teacher ...

In England as a contract accountant, corporate trainer, estate manager, lecturer, singer/songwriter, website editor/writer and freelance writer …

Now that I'm back in Australia, house renovating, teaching and writing, I'm wondering what's next!

The constant for my wife and I is *A Course in Miracles*, a psychological life-style course in forgiveness. Through it I have found the peace I had always been searching for - the journey to where we have always been.

Spleen ...

Philip J Bradbury in social media
About Me: https://about.me/philipbradbury
Amazon: amzn.to/25X0CLb
Facebook:
https://www.facebook.com/AuthorPhilipJBradbury/
Google+: http://bit.ly/2bsbpUy
Linked In: http://bit.ly/2aTzZMS
PinInterest: https://au.pinterest.com/bradburywords/
Smashwords: http://bit.ly/2aNjkic
Twitter: https://twitter.com/PhilipJBradbury
Website: www.philipjbradbury.com
Wordpress blogs:
https://flashfictionfanatic.wordpress.com/
https://pjbradbury.wordpress.com/

Other books by Philip J Bradbury

Non-Fiction

Whose Life Is It Anyway?
The Lawless Way
Change Your Life, Change Your World
The Twelve Week Miracle (with Anna Bradbury)
Understanding Men
Articles of Faith
Conversations on Your Business
Stepping Out Of Debt and Into Financial Freedom

Some-Fiction

Dactionary – the dictionary with attitude
The Meaning of Larf

Fiction

An Olympic Challenge
The Royal Bank of Stories
Circles of Gold
Gerald the Great of Gorokoland

Words in progress - looking for a publisher

40 Moments With Writing
42 Moments With Men
50 Moments With Fables
55 Moments With God
65 Moments With Self
22 Moments With Odes
The Last Stand-Down
The Last Accusation
The Last Expulsion

For more information on these books, see
www.philipjbradbury.com

53 SMILES

53
Special
Moments
In Life's
Exquisite
Simplicity

Philip J Bradbury

Published by The Write Site,
Brisbane, Australia

ISBN- 978-0-9922908-5-6

Thank you ...

I am able to put these intangible ideas into words and Anna, my wife, is able to put them into action; the reason she's such a good life coach. She is my best friend and greatest inspiration and I thank her from the bottom of my beating heart for being there, for loving me and for being that which I wish for myself.

Anna edited this book with her razor eye for the details I didn't see.

Thank you also to Tracie Louise for her beautiful cover photograph. You can see more of Tracie Louise's photographs at http://tracielouise.com.

I am also indebted to *A Course in Miracles* - and all the people I have met through it - for it shows me the way to peace; that way that is both simple and difficult. Forgiveness is simple but it's difficult to do in every second of our lives.

I keep trying ...

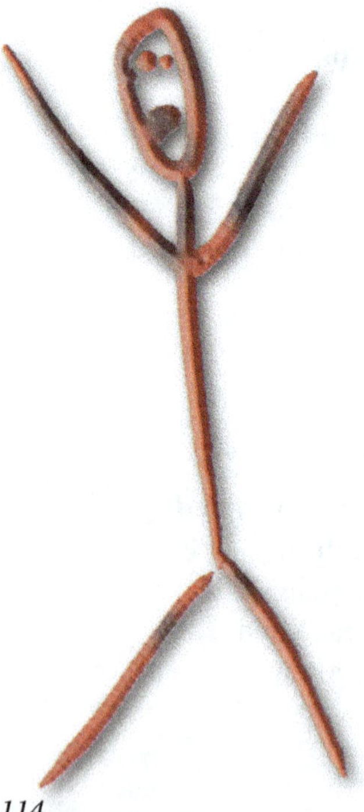

53 SMILES is about life – your life, my life, our liv
and its tiny stories address the big questions of
human condition and tell of our simple greatne
our foibles and how to let go of the need to
something for somebody else. This book, th
has many uses ...

- As an exquisitely simple gift,
- As a coffee table book,
- Conversation starter,
- Daily meditations,
- Personal/spiritual development workshops,
- Life Coaching,
- Table topics for Toastmasters,
- Teaching children (of any age) life lessons,
- To remind you of who you are each day – simply exquisite!

The wording is poetic and beautifully written. This book is best del
into rather than being read from cover to cover and is less about be
entertained and more about being challenged to grow persona
~ Anna Louise, life coach

Short and to the point yet insightful. If contemplated at depth t
can provide insights to the spirit of who we are as humans. Like
signposts in life, the stories contained in 53 SMILES can help you m
in a direction and place to finding joy. Some are comical some are
but all provide the reader with a plethora of ideas to ponder."
Julian Harvey, career consultant

www.ingramcontent.com/pod-product-compliance
Lightning Source LLC
Chambersburg PA
CBHW070314120726
47910CB00007B/2481
9780992290856